This Little Tiger book belongs to:

_____

_____

To Mark, Jess, Joe, and James

– J H

For Clarice Mary Alice and Vera Maud

– C P

LITTLE TIGER PRESS
1 The Coda Centre, 189 Munster Road,
London SW6 6AW
www.littletiger.co.uk

First published in Great Britain 2014
This edition published 2015

Text copyright © Julia Hubery 2014
Illustrations copyright © Caroline Pedler 2014

Julia Hubery and Caroline Pedler have asserted their rights to be
identified as the author and illustrator of this work under the
Copyright, Designs and Patents Act, 1988

A CIP catalogue record for this book is
available from the British Library

Printed in China • LTP/1400/1157/0515

2 4 6 8 10 9 7 5 3 1

When Granny Saved Christmas

Julia Hubery * Caroline Pedler

LITTLE TIGER PRESS
London

"Yippeeee! It's nearly Christmas!" sang Bubble.
"And we're going to Granny's!" added Squeak
as he helped Mummy pack his snowflake pyjamas.
"Hurry up then," smiled Mummy, "it's a long drive!"
"I wish we could fly to Granny's," sighed Bubble,
"like Santa in his sleigh."

"Oh no, Bubble!" Squeak cried. "How will Santa know we're at Granny's? He might come here!"

"Easy-peasy!" said Bubble. "We'll tell him!"

"We'll scooter to Lapland,

pogo over the penguins, and hitch a polar-bear ride to the North Pole!"

"Wow, have we got time for
all that?" said Mummy.
"How about writing Santa
a letter?"

"Clever Mummy!" said Squeak
as they got to work. "Let's make
it really BIG!"

"So Santa sees it!" agreed Bubble.

With snowy sparkles and
glittery glue, they made the
most magnificent letter ever.

"I wrote Santa's address HUGE, to make sure it gets there," Bubble told Squeak as Daddy helped them post the letter.

But just as it plopped through the slot, Squeak cried, "Bubble! We forgot to tell Santa Granny's address. How will he know where to go?"

"I know!" said Bubble.

"We'll bake a bazillion carrotty cookies . . .

and leave a trail for Rudolph to follow!"

"Sounds yummy!" said Daddy,
as they whizzed home.
"But Granny's waiting
to see us. Could we
just leave Santa
a map?"

"Clever Daddy!" said Squeak.

Together they helped
Daddy draw a map,

and pin it to the door.

Then they helped Mummy
pack the car.

"Hooray! We're off to Granny's!"
everyone cheered, as they
squashed the boot shut.

On the way they counted Christmas trees.

"I've seen two! Six! Twenty!" yelled Bubble.

"I've seen eighty-numpty-nine!" cried Squeak.

"That's not a number!" Bubble giggled.

"It is, IT IS – isn't it, Daddy?" shouted Squeak.

"Are we nearly there yet?" sighed Daddy.

At last they saw Granny's house
sparkling in the snow.

"Grannyyyy!" yelled Bubble and Squeak,
jumping into a big Granny-hug.

"My favourite little mice!" she beamed.

Then, Bubble suddenly
stopped.

"OH NO!" he gasped,
staring at Granny's roof.

"Granny, where's your chimney?"
cried Bubble.

"There isn't one!" squeaked Squeak.
"How will Santa get in?"
they both wailed.

"Don't worry," smiled Granny.
"I've been very busy while I was
waiting for you. "

Bubble and Squeak followed Granny
into her garden.

"Wow!" they gasped.

"It's my Super-swishy-Santa-Slide!"
said Granny.

"Clever Granny!" cheered Squeak.

"Santa's sure to find us now!"
cried Bubble.

THIS WAY, SANTA!

The little mice swooped and swished down Santa's Slide until the stars began to twinkle, and Granny called, "Cocoa-time!"

After cocoa and kisses, they wriggled
into their pyjamas, and Granny read
them a bedtime story.

"Thanks for making sure Santa
   finds us, Bubble," yawned Squeak
as the pair snuggled down to sleep.
"I hope he brings you a lovely
   present."

And guess what . . .

. . . Santa did!

Cuddle up in your Christmas jim-jams and share these wonderful books!

Waiting for Santa
Steve Metzger · Alison Edgson

Is It Christmas Yet?
Jane Chapman

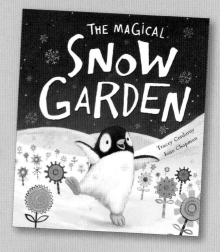

THE MAGICAL SNOW GARDEN
Tracey Corderoy · Jane Chapman

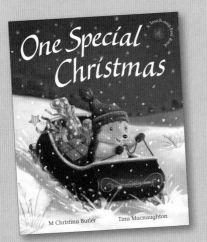

One Special Christmas
A Touch-and-Feel Book
M Christina Butler · Tina Macnaughton

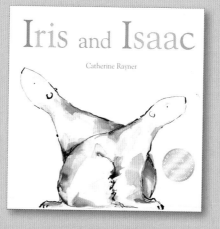

Iris and Isaac
Catherine Rayner

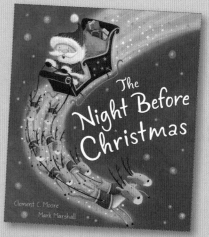

The Night Before Christmas
Clement C. Moore · Mark Marshall

For information regarding
any of the above titles or
for our catalogue, please contact us:
Little Tiger Press, 1 The Coda Centre,
189 Munster Road, London SW6 6AW
Tel: 020 7385 6333
E-mail: contact@littletiger.co.uk
www.littletiger.co.uk